The Deaths of Henry King

Art Direction by Tom Kaczynski

Uncivilized Books
P.O. Box 6534
Minneapolis, MN 55406
USA
uncivilizedbooks.com

First Edition, October 2017

10 9 8 7 6 5 4 3 2 1

ISBN 978-1-941250-20-4

DISTRIBUTED TO THE TRADE BY:
Consortium Book Sales & Distribution, LLC.
34 Thirteenth Avenue NE, Suite 101
Minneapolis, MN 55413-1007
cbsd.com, Orders: (800) 283-3572

Printed in Korea

The Deaths of
Henry King

Jesse Ball
Brian Evenson
Lilli Carré

Uncivilized Books

)))

From the moment you understand that... dying means nothing, that after death one continues to speak and to act as though no border had been crossed, and also that one can die several times in different ways, from the moment you admit that as a logic, you can travel easily in my books.

—ANTOINE VOLODINE

1

Henry King woke with a hammer partway through his head. Someone pulled the end of the hammer out of the hole and then brought it down again, causing Henry's body to shake a little all over, especially at the extremities.

2

Henry King was asked to meet a friend in a park. He went there and was killed. That same day, a bit later on, someone left an envelope on his doorstep. It wasn't a very fancy envelope, yet neither was it the absolutely cheapest kind.

3

Henry King signed a piece of paper that said, "I want to die." On 42nd and 5th a bus ran him over and he was so unremarkable, even at that moment, that a dozen more cars hit him before anyone thought to stop.

4

Henry King was burned to death in a house fire although many others were saved. "There is still someone in there," said the Fire Chief.

5

Henry King was riding a bus when he had two heart attacks. While he was curling up dead, someone made a petty observation about the cloth of his shirt, which was badly soiled.

Henry King was found by his dog, who later ate him. The dog escaped out a window and made his way west.

7

Henry King's blonde hair was a bad sign, the doctor told him. "Prone to lightning strikes and drowning. That sort of thing." In fact, two years later, he was hit by lightning while walking on a promenade. No one else in the crowd was even injured.

Henry King fell from an open window. A girl was telling a joke about a platypus. It was an extremely funny joke, and many kept laughing, even when they saw what had happened.

9

Henry King stayed late at the factory. His legs were caught in the machinery and it embarrassed him. The factory was sold by the owner that night and no one ever came back on to the premises, leaving Henry to death by starvation.

10

Henry King's costume was exhibited at the zoo where he died. Never wear such clothing at the zoo, a sign said.

11

Henry King accepted a drink from a wild-eyed girl underneath a bridge. Some minutes later, she was rolling over his body and removing an antique watch, the gift of his grandfather.

12

Henry King climbed a ladder and then it began to rain. By chance all the rain went into his mouth and he drowned before he could fall.

13

Henry King rounded a corner and watched someone get beaten to death by fifteen men. He did not see the whole thing, though, because the name of the person who was beaten to death was Henry King.

14

Henry King couldn't breathe. His throat had closed. He ran to the window and waved to someone outside. He slapped at his neck and chest with his hand. He waved to someone else who waved back and even smiled, yes, smiled.

15

Henry King wrote a suicide note on his shirt. It said, "I am sorry, Gertrude, but I had to bury myself alive."

16

Henry King was deep in a mine when the workers' canaries started to perish. Soon, the canary on the cage on his belt, it too perished. He had time to do one last thing.

17

Henry King became a leper by accident after visiting an old friend, a recluse, repeatedly for years in a basement apartment. Yes, leprosy, said the doctor. I don't know where you could have gotten it.

Henry King ate six and a half pounds of glass before bleeding to death. "I believe that's a record," said his friend.

19

Henry King fell down the stairs in a building nearby. There wasn't a mark on him. "You would think he had survived," said a girl.

20

Henry King's death was judged a heart attack by the first detective, who deciphered his handwritten note to read "Good Biker Gruel". The second deciphered it as "Goodbye Cruel World" and changed cause of death to suicide. A third has been called in to break the tie.

Nobody knew how Henry King had come to be in Little Chute during the Great Wisconsin Cheese Festival, nor why, when the giant wheel of cheddar broke its moorings, he did not at least try to jump out of the way.

Henry King realized mid-leap that the other building's roof was in fact much farther away than he'd realized.

23

It was a mystery how Henry King's car had gotten onto the supermarket roof, but much less of a mystery than why he had spontaneously combusted.

Henry King's last gasping thought was that they should change the maxim "Don't put anything smaller than your elbow in your ear" to "Don't put anything smaller than an elbow in your ear, especially not a knitting needle."

All that remained of Henry King after his fall from the balloon was a Henry King shaped dent in the ground. Soon that was gone as well.

"Quelled by a q-tip?" was the unlikely title of the article on the unlikely death of Henry King.

In the blizzard, Henry King froze to death just ten feet from his owndoor. A pack of dogs dragged the body farther away, in pieces and in all directions.

A small smudge in a painting by Breughel was discovered to be the image of none other than Henry King, killed in a threshing accident by a man with a cow's head, no relation to the famous explorer.

Henry King discovered that the inside of Henry King looks like any meat one might buy at a butcher's shop. He smiled wryly, and perished.

Henry King argued fruitlessly with Charon. I have no money. You must have some money. I have no money. You must have some money. I have no money. You must...

Henry King wore a special shirt for people who may be one day kidnapped. This made him more comfortable in day to day life. He bought special shoes for people who need to survive short falls. He wore an actual helmet. He covered his crotch with a semi-articulated neoprene and steel codpiece. This odd appearance was sufficient to provoke a mob in Buenos Aires, where he was killed while attempting to enter a soccer stadium. Thirty people stood on his head until it was flat. They left his body alone.

A man by the name of Henry King was killed by a folk song about a man named Henry King (not he) that implicated a Henry King in a murder in Baton Rouge of which he (Henry King) was innocent, but for which he (Henry King) was eventually tried and executed.

A bullet had the word Henry scratched into it. Another bullet, the word King. Someone loaded these into a revolver and then put the weapon down on a table covered in loose change and various ornaments. A doorbell rang. Someone who was sleeping woke up.

"Heinrich Konig?" asked the man with the expressionless face as he pointed the Ruger LC9 at his skull. "Henry King," corrected Henry King, shaking same head. But the dark-suited man had already pulled the trigger.

35

In space, nobody can hear your scream. In addition, Henry King discovered, when you try to scream, your lungs collapse and your saliva seems to boil. You experience seizures and pitting edema and briefly have the impression that ants are crawling over your skin. And then your lips and mouth freeze. At no point in the process is it possible to let out a scream.

36

Henry King must have taken a wrong turn somewhere, for he was
not to be found among those who had successfully navigated the
river and now floated on the lake, cans of Schlitz balanced on their
bellies. Instead his tube popped, he was swept along by currents and
bashed by rocks until his corpse was caught in a backwater. It lay there
bloating in the company of his own can of Schlitz, which, thanks to
the water, was ice-cold.

37

To defuse the situation the officer fired his gun into the ceiling, which collapsed and brought about the demise of Henry King.

The bottles in the cellar were delicately balanced. Removing the '45 Chateau Margaux brought all the other bottles cascading down on Henry King. He lay there half-crushed and badly cut, dying, stinking of expensive wine.

39

It was a mistake to try to separate the two fighting pit bulls. Henry King was fairly certain both of them bit him repeatedly, but was in no condition to ascertain which one tore his throat out.

Henry King reached into his bag. "I believe this is what you're looking for." The man with the pale shadow flayed Henry then and there. The flaying was painful and it took quite a while. That's what it is, thought Henry, dying. That's what it is! His shadow, too, is wearing a shadow made of skin.

Henry King's hat was to be removed for the sculpting of the deathmask. "No, no, I insist," said someone. "He always wore it. Always. It must remain." Never mind that Henry had no hat, that there was no sculptor, not even a bystander to speak at all. Still, the hat was removed, the objection noted. "All tears for the widow," said the sculptor, as if that solved anything.

42

Henry King's body was found face down on the sidewalk, dead. It seems that stepping on a crack had broken his own back rather than that of his mother.

43

Henry King would have been fine if he'd gone to the doctor rather than covering up the wound with an old ace bandage. By the time he unwrapped it, the foot was gangrenous, shrunken, and blackly red. He might still have been all right, had he not attempted to save money by performing the amputation himself, at home, with a band saw.

Henry King perished when an enormous pile of hats fell on him in his father's hat factory. At the time, he was only a child. His father, man of hats that he was, had the boy made into a fine Stetson hat, which he wore for many years with great pleasure.

Oh, look there. A commotion of sorts. Henry King's foot is caught in a "moving staircase," which some call an escalator. The natives turn on him immediately, stripping his still living body of all valuables, including clothing. One begins to eat his ear and cheek, crouching over him. Astonishing behavior!

46

Henry King died of the kissing disease. Those he knew preferred not to speak of it.

Henry King played a game called "clouds and jewels" with the cooks in a sinister Chinese restaurant after the usual mahjong game was over with. This "clouds and jewels," as they called it, involved eating small bits of one thing disguised as another and guessing what was what. At least, that's how the First Cook explained it to the detective, as they stood there in the harsh fluorescent light of the kitchen, looking down on Henry King's corpse, where it rested beneath the filthy card table. "I know what you mean," said the detective, carelessly.

"Henry" King, in reality Henriette, leaned her musket against one wall of the dilapidated French fort, removed her regimental coat, laid her cocked hat on a chair and shook out her long hair. "What will history think of me?" she wondered. At that moment a French light infantryman who had been disguised as a pair of candlesticks stood up on the table and shot her through the face with an outdated heirloom arquebus, some sort of matchlock, one might say. That a man who would disguise himself as a candlestick should have such a weapon... it is inevitable, thought Henriette, and promptly perished.

49

According to 12th Century parish records, the King had been accosted by a smiling man who claimed his name "to be a reverse of thine own, sire. Thou art King Henry, and I am Henry King." King Henry's response was to have Henry King beheaded.

50

Henry King reasoned that if one Viagra pill worked well, ten would work even better. Eighteen hours and two Houses of Ill Repute later, his heart gave out.

51

The Henricus Kingicus fungus, named after its first victim, is perfectly adapted to the urban environment: its roughly rectangular shape resembles a cheap cell phone seemingly dropped just off the edge of a sidewalk. When touched, it collapses into thousands of deadly airborne spores. Death comes almost immediately. Experts agree it is an evolutionary marvel.

52

Henry King seemed to have been turned to stone. There was a great deal of consternation among his neighbors: half believed he had been petrified, the other half believed he had made a statue of himself and then left town. Discussion became argument and argument became fisticuffs, and in the brawl that followed Henry King, or his representation, was knocked over and broken to pieces.

Henry King went to Hokkaido to see the cherry blossoms, never mind that there are better ones elsewhere, it was to Hokkaido he went. And quite simply, the visit was too much for him. Even these so to speak Hokkaido cherry blossoms, they were too intense, too perfect, too redolent of life's equal measure of splendor and strife: he collapsed on the spot, clutching at his chest. "I confess!" he cried, beginning a sentence he would never end.

54

Henry King, world traveller, sat staring at his plate. There was, he was fairly certain, a snout, a foot as well, a gummy ear edged with a threadline of dark bristles. If they can eat it, it must be all right, he told himself, and dug in to the meal that, months later, would end up being the death of him.

At the bottom of the stairs was the corpse of an old woman. Some neighborhood kids were up to the old hijinks, pissing on it and hitting it with sticks. Then the police chief arrived on the scene. "That's no old woman. It's the body of Henry King, the renowned astronomer."

His last memory as Henry King was the stick coming down toward his face. It was followed as if without transition by the smiling face of a nurse, but by then he had lost track of his name and never quite managed to retrieve it.

Henry King was an extra in an Andy Warhol film in which the twenty prettiest girls in New York City climbed up a ladder and fell off into the East River. The last one fucked it up really badly so Andy Warhol said get the next prettiest thing on the set up that ladder pronto and Henry King was next prettiest but couldn't swim. They made him go anyway.

58

Henry King had seen the open manhole from some distance away. Must be careful, he thought, remembering incidents from his pasts. He approached the manhole slowly, always keeping it in sight, and then, very cautiously, stepped over it and into the path of a speeding bus.

59

Henry King had a dream in which he was the figurehead of a tremendous sailing ship. He was plunging through the churning seas and then the unthinkable came — the ship was sinking. The ship was sunk. A boy with a drill had swum alongside and drilled and drilled his heart out until he had made a hole the size of his hand, and that was enough. As Henry King sank with his ship he remembered something he had once heard said: if you dream your way to the bottom of the sea, if you dream you are a statue at the bottom of the sea, then you will never wake, and your loved ones will peel the covers back from your corpse and bear your body into another room. He wished fervently he had not heard that as the ship settled into the sediment and little streams of fish fled past his unmoving eyes.

Henry King offended the bus driver of his schoolbus. When his stop came, the bus driver prevented him from getting off. This continued until he was too weak even to attempt to leave the bus. All the children would laugh at him as he sheltered there in the rut beside the wheel well. I will die in the springtime, thought Henry, with everything growing. But he was mistaken; he perished in January when the bus was parked in a snowdrift for a week. By that time he was so small and weak, he was not even capable of having his remains found. Instead, the bus driver swept him from the bus with a broom, singing some idiotic little song known only to bus drivers.

After several narrow escapes and a harrowing experience with a man holding under his arm what Henry initially thought was a soccer ball but quickly realized was a human head, Henry King stumbled through the jungle and onto the airstrip. Crouching, he ran across the tarmac and clambered into the plane's wheel well. At last he was safe. A few minutes later the plane took off and the wheel crushed him.

"Henry King, you say," said the grizzled old man to the investigating officer. "He never told me his name but I suppose it must be him. You'll find him at the bottom of that," he said, and pointed with the stem of his pipe to the edge of the ravine.

In the dream Henry King was thrown free of the car and, though badly injured and comatose for weeks, he did manage to survive and go on to marry, have children, and have grandchildren, finally dying peacefully at a ripe old age. In reality, Henry King, asleep at the wheel, was killed instantly when his car crossed into the other lane and struck a semi head on.

Henry King's girlfriend had left him for a weedy, tattooed alcoholic ex-punk singer working a minimum wage job. What has he got that I haven't got? wondered Henry King. He starved himself until he was rail thin. He covered his body with tattoos and took a job as a janitor. He wrote thirty songs, each less than a minute long, and then screamed them into a microphone while backed by the band he had started, Cradle of Flies, then quit the band. Still she didn't come back. He lay in his apartment, drinking vodka, waiting for her return until he was too weak to leave, slowly wasting away.

65

When the rain came it was not rain at all, but a pale scouring of dust or sand. Henry King watched it strip the paint off the car and slowly grind the windscreen opaque. And then he made the mistake of opening the car door.

An angel came to Henry King in a dream and showed him his eternal lot: a sun black but shining, a cataract of blood shot through with fire. "And what is this a metaphor for?" asked Henry King. "It is no metaphor," said the angel. "And when shall it befall me?" asked Henry King. "Now," said the angel, and reached down his throat and tore out his heart.

The phone call came late at night. "You've been activated," said a flat, expressionless voice. "Excuse me?" said Henry King. "The puppy is out of the crate," said the voice. "But I don't have a puppy," said Henry King. There was a long pause. "Incorrect," said the voice. "You will be terminated." "Terminated?" said Henry King. "Hello?" But the line was already dead.

Estranged from his children and separated from his wife, Henry King went camping alone. The island was deserted, peaceful, quiet. He had time to think through his mistakes. He was already envisioning a better life when the bear ate him.

Henry King appeared in an old print, entitled, The Making of Useful Artifacts. He was holding a useful artifact and being whipped by a satyr. The accompanying text said, "so perished the ryghte honrable Henree Kin, betrayde by all his friends, large and small, of meadow and spring."

Henry King named his hat Henry King. He beheld it and growled. Suddenly, he snatched it up. He tore out the hatband. He used his fingers as scissors, obscenely to separate the fine weaves. He bit at it with his agate mouth agape. He chewed the dome and swallowed, swallowed, failed to swallow, reached into his own mouth, but never deep enough or quickly enough, and soon was dead of his own hat, and of his own campaign to end his hat. So perished, doubly, Henry King.

Henry King was the name the guerrillas had for any of the corpse decoys they would leave floating out on the river. When the national forces would try to salvage a corpse, the partisans would blow it up, demolishing watercraft and would-be salvager. Why the corpse decoys were called Henry Kings–there were a few theories. An old rebel said they were named after Henry VIII because of all his wives–in this case the boats the exploding corpse destroyed. Another said this was nonsense. "Henry King's just a British word for water mammals–otters, walrus, sea lions what have you." When an uncomfortable silence ensued, he took it back. "Leastways, I know a man named Henry and he looked mostly like an otter. Leastways, I used to know him."

Henry King, memorialized as the man who discovered, though realizing it only too late to do him any good, that certain breeds of otters can become carnivorous when subjected to habitat stress and change. The consumption of Henry King by otters as documented by a Japanese tourist's video camera, is, according to noted scientist Heinrich von Helldorf, invaluable in understanding the darker side of our furry little friends.

It is a little known custom of the natives of certain Polynesian islands to claim for themselves the name, "Henry King," on their deathbeds. The origins of this curious tradition are unknown, but thought to date back to serviceman Henry King, a US Navy pilot, who perished there in the 1940s.

Even yesterday, I tell you, all evening long in the hospital ward: "I am Henry King."

"Call me Henry King."

"Henry King, I say it, my name."

And the dutiful nurses emerge from behind curtains to gently confirm each claim.

"You are Henry King," they say. "You are. You are a certain Henry King."

74

And so they took a newborn lamb, of fair appearance and with white and unblemished fleece and then slit its throat and gathered the blood in a bowl made of hammered brass. And then they took a bunch of hyssop and dipped it in the bowl and spread the blood on the posts, and upon the lintel wrote in blood the words "Henry King." And thereafter they closed the door and did not open it until morning. And thus it was that the angel of death passed them by, but throughout the city and throughout the world, during that night and for all their nights thereafter, they were afflicted by the sounds of Henry King, dying.

The waiting room is very long. You enter it by a small door that appears little used. Then, as far as the eye can see, chairs, benches, tables stretching into the distance: an unintelligibly long line of people quietly waiting. No one looks at you. Their thoughts occupy them. They have been waiting forever. You are now waiting, too. But no sooner do you sit down than a voice is calling to you. Someone has come to a partition of sorts and is calling to you. A man in a well-sewn suit of immaculate cloth is calling something out. He is calling to you.

"King, Henry. King, Henry. Henry King. This way."

Uncomprehending looks then from the incidentally limitless queue of claimants. They are peering now at you, lowering newspapers, spectacles, raising eyebrows, fans, gesturing. This is unheard of. Someone is being called. You are being called. Unheard of.

"Henry King..."

You raise your arm, push through the throng to the makeshift gate that is all that's holding back this sea of listless humanity that now is groaning, waking.

"Let him through."

Someone takes you quite literally by the nape of the neck and lifts you up. You are being carried through the air. You are young again. It is meaningless, and you begin to cry. You are dead and you have never been so happy.

There is a house, modest and unassuming, on the edge of our town, which having remained unoccupied for years has become more than a house. We only visit it when we are tired of life but do not have the courage to bring about our own demise. If you go to the door and knock and then position your lips near the letter slot and repeat the words "Henry King" three times, then you will hear a belowground rustling, the gentle knocking of a fist on a narrow window, then the slow sound of footsteps climbing the cellar stairs. If you peek through the letter slot you will see nothing, but you will hear a body approaching and will sense it just there, unseen and unseeable, on the other side of the door, waiting. Now you must say: "Henry King, I take your death upon me," and then turn away from the door without awaiting reply. Then Death will come after you--in a few hours, a few days, a few years--thinking you are not yourself, but rather poor Henry King.

At security, Henry King found he had forgotten to bring the note from his doctor, and had his inhaler taken away. On the plane he was seated next to a woman trained as a nurse, and when he began to have trouble breathing she did her best to talk him through it. Breathe through your nose, honey. Breathe through your nose, she kept saying in a voice so calm and so relaxed that he was surprised, when he opened his eyes, to see so much fear gathered in her face. His breathing grew worse and worse. An emergency landing was made, but by the time they touched down, he was already dead.

Henry King rode the glass elevator up to the 31st floor so that he could look out and see the lights and the enormous Christmas tree in the square. In the brief pause between when the doors opened and the doors closed again, he could not help but imagine what it would be like to fall from this height, to go tumbling down the side of the building and flash into the ground below. It came to him so vividly that for an instant he felt he was living hand in hand with his own death. Then the doors closed and he rode the elevator down again and walked home alone.

The path wound slowly along the narrow spit of land and through undergrowth and trees. Here there was a damp earthy smell and there the woody tang of eucalyptus. Henry King could see the waves below, the sound of them more distant than he felt it should be. A path led down to beach but was blocked off with police tape and a warning. He ignored both. At first the going was easy, then more difficult, then the sides of the path crumbled and gave way and Henry King began to scramble back up. And then the whole path went, and he along with it.

Henry King had said goodbye to Henry King so many times that all the stationery was used up. If he were such a one as would think of that sort of thing, Henry King would have said to himself, I believe no one has ever used up so many ink pots in saying goodbye. But he was not. He led a band of Indians to their deaths in a ravine surrounded by soldiers. By that I mean he fed himself into a boiler in the basement of an old building and was scalded like something your grandmother used to cook in the days when everything was cooked "just so." Goodnight!

Henry King was speaking with Carl Jung about the enormous spiritual distress of his situation. "Nonetheless," said King, "I feel I am not a victim." "But perhaps symbolically..." suggested Jung quietly. "Symbolically, yes, I suppose," admitted King, "symbolically, one must begin to admit, I suppose." Jung leaned back, using his enormous furry chest to make the sign of St. Michael. Henry King wept softly then, eagerly, rashly, as if he were in a hat store, and behind him on the wall, a mounted bird let out some final, impossible cry.

Henry King asked one of the girls to bring another girl. Bring another girl he said. They brought another girl. He said to her bring another girl. Bring another girl he said. They brought another girl. They brought another girl and another girl and another girl. Finally they were there, all of the girls. All of the girls were there. I don't know what to do with you, said Henry King. You may, said the girls, do what you like to every one of us, but it will certainly kill you. You will do what you like, almost certainly, and certainly it will kill you.

Henry King felt his way along the crack in the bathroom wall. He slowly wormed his finger into it, though to do so stripped his finger to the bone. His hand followed, then his wrist, then his whole arm. To make the rest of his body fit, he had to pound it flat by beating the body repeatedly with a cast- iron pan. After that, though, it was easy. Before he knew it he was back behind the crack. But it was too dark to see what, if anything, was there, and though he had managed to work his way in, he did not have the same success working his way back out.

Zlata the Ukrainian had a habit of allowing herself to be bent double during intercourse, the inner curve of her feet gently cradling each side of Henry King's neck. Remarkable, Henry King thought, not realizing that she was simply biding her time for the moment when the prearranged signal would flash through the window and with a quick twist of her ankles she would break his neck.

85

There came a time when Henry King found he could not recognize himself in the mirror. Yes, admittedly there was someone there, a reversed creature staring back from the glass. And yet, no matter how much he tried to invest himself in the image, he could not see himself in it. It was as if he were watching another man who was wearing Henry King's skin. Was this Henry King or was it not? And if not, what had become of him?

Gently Henry King nudged each flea into place on his arm, allowing it to feed. He returned them one by one to their places, careful not to confuse them. Then, humming, he lay on his side in the bed, the skin of his arm itching, watching the tiny miracle of this blood-fueled circus.

87

There are so many ways to die, thought Henry King, and nearly as many ways to live.

A man roots through uniforms in an enormous military commissary, now defunct. He sees a bright blue parade coat, dressed with white ribbon and fine gray felt like a mouse's belly. It is the uniform of the Henry Kings, that long forgotten battalion of the Welsh Fusiliers, decimated at Flanders never to recover. "Thus," recalls the man to himself aloud, "veterans once would say at parades, 'leave the rearguard to the Henry Kings, though they shall be long in coming.'"

At the morgue, Henry King! At the fair, Henry King! At the air show, Henry King! It was the Henry King holiday, November 9th, and everyone was dressed up as Henry King and ready to die in some new obscene and incomprehensible way. Meanwhile, Henry King skulked amidst the machinery of fate, pulling here a lever, there a string.

Jesse Ball is the author of five novels, including *A Cure for Suicide* (Pantheon 2015), *Silence Once Begun* and *The Curfew*, and several works of verse, bestiaries, and sketchbooks. He is the recipients of numerous awards, including a 2014 NEA Creative Writing Fellowship and the 2008 Paris Review George Plimpton Prize, and his verse has been included in *The Best American Poetry* series. He gives classes on lucid dreaming and lying in the School of the Arts Institute of Chicago's MFA Writing program.

Lilli Carré is an interdisciplinary artist and illustrator currently living in Chicago. Her animated films have shown in festivals throughout the US and abroad, including the Sundance Film Festival, and she is the co-founder of the Eyeworks Festival of Experimental Animation. She has created several books of comics, most recently the short story collection, *Heads or Tails*, published by Fantagraphics, and her first children's book, *Tippy and the Night Parade*, published by Toon Books. Her work has appeared in the *New Yorker*, *The New York Times*, *Best American Comics* and *Best American Nonrequired Reading*, amongst other places. Solo exhibitions of her drawing, animation, and sculpture work were recently on display at the Museum of Contemporary Art Chicago and the Columbus Museum of Art in 2014.

Brian Evenson is the author of a dozen books of fiction, most recently the story collection *Windeye* and the novel *Immobility*, both of which were finalists for a Shirley Jackson Award. His novel *Last Days* won the American Library Association's RUSA award for Best Horror Novel of 2009. His novel *The Open Curtain* was a finalist for an Edgar Award and an International Horror Guild Award. Other books include *The Wavering Knife* (which won the IHG Award for best story collection), *Dark Property*, and *Altmann's Tongue*. He is the recipient of three O. Henry Prizes as well as an NEA fellowship. His work has been translated into French, Italian, Spanish, Japanese and Slovenian. He livesin Providence, Rhode Island, where he teaches in Brown University's Literary Arts Department.

UNCIVILIZED BOOKS CATALOGUE

The Voyeurs by Gabrielle Bell

Truth is Fragmentary by Gabrielle Bell

Everything is Flammable by Gabrielle Bell

An Iranian Metamorphosis by Mana Neyestani

Incidents in the Night Book One & Two by David B.; Translated by Brian Evenson

Amazing Facts & Beyond by Kevin Huizenga & Dan Zettwoch

War of Streets and Houses by Sophie Yanow

Post York by James Romberger & Crosby

It Never Happened Again by Sam Alden

Plans We Made by Simon Moreton

Eel Mansions by Derek Van Gieson

Over the Wall by Peter Wartman

Sammy The Mouse by Zak Sally

True Swamp by Jon Lewis

Pascin by Joann Sfar; Translated by by Edward Gauvin

Borb by Jason Little

CRITICAL CARTOONS SERIES:

Ed vs. Yummy Fur by Brian Evenson

Carl Bark' Duck by Peter Schilling Jr.

Brighter Than You Think by Alan Moore, with essays by Marc Sobel

and more...

uncivilizedbooks.com